Dingus Slopp and The Portapotty Palace
The Flippin' Mud Festival

By: DeNaze Wharton
Contributors:
Jacob Jones
Kayden Polidan
Illustrations: D. Wharton

CHAPTER 1

SPECKS AND PORTIES

"Everything. It's going to change."

"Dingus Slopp!" called out Mrs. Slopp.

Dingus scootered as fast as his ten-year-old legs could take him. He weaved in and around the green, blue, and red portable toilets trying to make it home as quickly as possible. He knew his way around ***Pooper's Portables*** so he took a shortcut behind the oval office.

The energetic, curly-haired, fourth-grader flew past EvyPoo Pott's Place, which was just around the corner from The Portapotty Palace where Dingus lived. The Pott's family was eating dinner at their picnic table. Dingus waved to his classmate as he went by.

"Hey Dingus, your mom's calling you!" EvyPoo said, mockingly.

"Big yikes," thought Dingus. "Why did his mom have to yell so loudly that everyone in *Pooper's Portables* could hear?"

Clayton Brown waved and made a weird face at Dingus when he passed the Brown's Bungalow. Dingus scootered faster and finally came to a halt right in front of The Portapotty Palace.

Mrs. Slopp was standing in the doorway. Seeing the look on her face, Dingus could tell he was in trouble, but he didn't know why. Maybe he had stayed too long at Stinky Johns' Jon. Mrs. Johns had invited him to eat some cookies after playing video games with Stinky. Maybe he left his backpack on the floor. Maybe he forgot to finish his chores after school.

That was it!

"Oh, poop!" said Dingus, when he suddenly remembered that he forgot to do the most important chore of all-the plunging!

"Oh, poop, is right!" Mom agreed.

Ever since Dingus was old enough to crank the valve, it was his job to hook up "The Mega Power Plunger" and plunge The Portapotty Palace.

Before Mom said another word, Dingus grabbed his mask and started flipping switches. The first switch always goes to the "off" position, the second switch to the "on" position and the third switch to the "on" position. It is very important that all of the switches are set correctly before plunging. If not, a major mishap could befall The Portapotty Palace. Dingus gave the big valve a crank.

"Let's go 'Bone Crusher!'" he said loudly.

In about fifteen-seconds, all the wastewater from The Portapotty Palace was sucked out and sent down the big, black hose to the sewer. After the plunge, a huge pressure wash went through and cleaned the main floor. The main floor of a portable toilet is called the poop deck, of course. In a flash, The Portapotty Palace was sparkling clean.

When the plunge and cleaning was complete, Dingus put all the switches back to the center and closed the valve. Blue, fresh smelling water filled each bowl in The Portapotty Palace.

In the portable toilet world, there are two kinds of people: specks and porties. "Specks" is short for spectators. They are the people who use the portable toilets at the events.

Specks usually don't know about porties. Porties are people who live in portable toilets. Most specks don't know that many portable toilets actually have three stories in them. A speck will just look for a green vacancy dial on the handle, use the poop deck and leave. They don't look around at the different doors and hatches right in front of them, above them, or under them. If specks looked up, they might see something that looks like a metal vent. It's really a staircase that collapses and pushes up when not in use. It leads up to the sleeping quarters.

If specks turned the dial on the door handle past the green section and past the red, they would see a blue triangle on the dial. When you turn the handle to blue, the poop deck floor opens to the lower deck. That's where the rest of the living quarters are found. It is where you would see the couch and television, and maybe a ping pong table or a gaming area. The lower deck is where the parents play poker, hoping for a royal flush.

"Toya, play 'Cow Patty Road'", Dingus announced to his cloud system. He pumped the foot pedal at the sanitation station pretending it was a bass drum. Dingus washed his hands an extra-long time hoping Mom would be calmed down. He had something important to ask her.

Dingus wanted to know if The Portapotty Palace was going to the school bus figure-eight races this weekend. Stinky's family was going and Dingus really wanted to go, also. The races are one of Dingus' favorite events. Last year, one bus clipped the back end of another bus, sending it into a spin. The bus crashed into a light pole. The light pole fell over and landed smack into a row of portables. Some people were screaming and freaking out while others were laughing when they saw no one was hurt. The Portapotty Palace came close to being demolished.

This weekend, some of **Pooper's Portables** were supposed to go to the school bus races and some were going to a concert. Mom's favorite singer was headlining the concert. He knew Mom wanted to go. But Dingus desperately wanted to go to the races with Stinky.

"Mom," said Dingus, in his sweetest voice. "Remember how much fun we always have at the school bus races? Could we please, please, please go back this year? I will do anything you need me to do. I promise I won't forget to plunge ever again. Please, Mom, pretty please?" Dingus begged.

Mom looked over at Dingus as she was grilling burgers, but said nothing. Pop was going to be home soon from his golf league. Dingus was setting out the silverware neatly on the picnic table, trying to be helpful. Maybe Mom would choose the races instead of her dumb old concert.

When Pop pulled up in the golf cart, Dingus could tell Pop had a good day on the golf course. He was smiling from ear to ear. Dingus thought this would be a good time to ask about going to the school bus races.

"How was golf today, Pop?" he asked, even though he could tell Pop did well.

"Holy smokes Gus! You should have seen it! Straight down the fairway, landing on the green, a foot away from the pin! My best drive ever!"

Dingus liked it when Pop called him Gus because he only called him Gus when he was in a good mood.

"Then a perfect putt into the cup!" Pop exclaimed as he washed his hands at the sanitation station. Dingus listened intently.

"Hey Gus," said Pop, "guess where The Portapotty Palace is going this weekend?"

His voice was so excited Dingus was sure Pop was going to say the school bus races!

"The races?" Dingus said excitedly, too.

"Sorry, son, not this weekend, there was a big switch at the oval office."

Dingus was taken by surprise.

"What?" Dingus' voice cracked. "We have to go to the concert?"

"Nope," replied Pop "we are going to the Flippin' Mud Festival!"

Dingus was disappointed. He and Stinky had been talking about the races for days. He had high hopes about hanging out with his best friend. Dingus had no idea what a Flippin' Mud Festival was about. But he did like the word mud.

CHAPTER 2

WHAT'S A FLIPPIN' MUD FESTIVAL?

"It's Muddy Fun!"

"What the heck is a Flippin' Mud Festival?" asked Dingus.

"Remember The Ultimate Mud Dare," replied Pop, "where they had the giant mud pond? It was awesome!"

Dingus thought for a second and remembered how the participants climbed up a giant wall at the end, then slid down slides and landed in a huge mud pit. They had to crawl through a pond of mud to get out. Dingus remembered EvyPoo actually lost her glasses because she slid super-fast and landed so hard into the mud that her glasses flew off her head. They were gone!

"I remember that," said Dingus. "What a mess!"

"The Flippin' Mud Festival is mud pits plus…" Pop said the word "plus" very slowly.

"Plus, a trampoline challenge!" Dad nearly shouted. He knew Dingus loved the trampolines and was the best jumper at *Pooper's Portables*.

"The best trampoline tricksters in the country are going to be there Gus, the guys you watch on your phone all the time! You can show them your stuff!" said Pop.

"Wow!" said Dingus. "That does sound pretty cool."

Pop grabbed one of the burgers Mom just made and started eating it, but then stopped when he could see something was wrong with Dingus.

"What's up, bud? What's the matter?"

"Well," Dingus stammered. "Um, that sounds pretty fun, Pop, I just hope Stinky's family can go, too."

"Oh, don't worry, Stinky's family is going. We are all going! Mr. Pooper was in the oval office today. He said *Pooper's* was outbid for the school bus races and the concert by *Superpoops*."

Pop gave Mom one of those looks that parents sometimes give each other. The one that says, "Don't let the kids know we are worried, but we are."

Mom looked back at Pop. This was the first she had heard about **Pooper's** losing the bid for the concert. Mom tried not to look surprised. She took a drink from her thermal water bottle that Dingus gave her for Mother's Day. It was red with a silhouette of The Portapotty Palace on the front.

"Stinky's going to the Flippin' Mud Festival, too? Sweet!" Dingus' mood changed quickly.

Stinky Johns and Dingus Slopp have been best friends for as long as they could remember. Believe it or not, Stinky and Dingus were born on the same day at the same hospital. They sometimes tell people they are twins just to prank them, but they aren't even brothers. Stinky has dark, straight hair like his dad and Dingus has curly, blondish hair like his mom. Stinky is tall and Dingus is on the smaller side.

Dingus wanted to be done eating so he could go back over to Stinky's and tell him about the trampoline mud festival.

"You need to finish eating that burger, Dingus," Mom said.

"But I can't wait to tell Stinky about this weekend!"

"You will be fine, kiddo, settle down" Mom replied.

Dingus shoved the last bite of his burger into his mouth, then grabbed his scooter and left for Stinky's house.

After Dingus was out of ear shot, Mom gave Pop a serious look. She was as surprised as anyone that two events were cancelled on one weekend. That rarely happens.

"So, what's going on up at the oval office?" Mom asked. "No one ever outbids *Pooper's!*"

"*Superpoops*" said Pop, as he settled into his zero-gravity chair.

"Apparently," he continued. "Mr. Swurlee, over at *Superpoops,* has upped his game and wants a bigger piece of the portable toilet pie. He hired a new marketing director named Constance Patience. She thinks *Superpoops* can put *Pooper's* right out of business. I guess she doesn't know Mr. Pooper has been in the portable toilet business for forty-five years. Everyone knows we have the cleanest portables and the softest tissue around."

"Something seems wrong about the whole situation, if you ask me," said Mom as she sat down next to Pop. "Something's just not right."

CHAPTER 3

GETTING READY

"Be prepared."

"Stinky!" called Dingus as he scootered toward his friend.

"Dingus!" Stinky yelled back as he picked up his scooter and headed toward Dingus.

"To the trampolines!" both boys yelled at the same time.

Stinky, who was tall and muscular for his age, was wearing his favorite camouflage hat and camouflage shorts that he always wore. Dingus usually didn't wear hats because everyone loved his big curly hair that his mom let him grow out. He was rather small for his age, so kids sometimes mistook him for younger than he was.

Although they were bummed about not getting to go to the school bus figure-eight races, they were both excited about the trampoline challenge. They were also excited that they might see their favorite vloggers at The Flippin' Mud Festival.

"I wonder if The Frog will be there?" Dingus said as they rounded the corner away from Stinky's house. The Frog was one of the best trampoline vloggers they watched. Like Dingus, The Frog could perform just about any trick on the trampolines on his first try.

They headed over to the trampoline yard. Mr. Pooper, the owner of *Pooper's Portables* loved the portie kids and built the area just for them. Excavators dug out the ground for three trampolines. Next to one of the trampolines was a wall for the portie kids to practice their wall tricks. Foam pits surround the trampolines.

Rhea, EvyPoo Pott's best friend, is very good on the trampolines, too. Rhea's mom, Diane, used to be an acrobat in the circus before coming to *Pooper's.* She taught the kids a lot of tricks on the trampolines.

When Stinky and Dingus scootered up, they heard hip-hop music playing on the speakers. One of the younger boys, Lou, hopped off the trampoline so Dingus could jump on. Dingus loved jumping and practiced his tricks every chance he got. The other portie kids loved watching him do his tricks and tried to imitate him.

Diane had shown Dingus how to do a flip when he was eight. He practiced over and over for two weeks straight. When Dingus finally mastered the flip, Diane taught him how to do a double. No one can do a double until they master the single. Dingus did it perfectly his first time. That is unusual for most kids.

When Stinky saw Dingus do a double, Stinky practiced and practiced but couldn't do it. The one thing Stinky was missing was confidence. When doing jumps and tricks on the trampoline, the first thing you need is confidence. Otherwise, you can just forget about it. Stinky was pretty good at other tricks like codys and kabooms, though.

"So, you all know we are going to the Flippin' Mud Festival this weekend, right?" Dingus said as he flipped and landed on his feet in front of Clayton Brown, a small and very quiet sixth grader.

Lou, who was six, piped up, "I wanted to go to the school bus races."

"*Pooper's* lost the bid," Dingus said as he stepped off the trampoline.

"Probably to *Superpoops*," Stinky said with a mocking tone.

"Go *Superpoops*!" said Clayton.

"Why did *Pooper's* lose the bid. Can we look for it?" Lou asked innocently.

The other portie kids chuckled.

"No, Lou," said EvyPoo Potts, "not lost that way. A bid is something that companies do to get a job they want. It's a piece of paper that Mr. Pooper gives to the event planner. It tells the planner how much they are going to charge to provide the portables for the event."

"If Mr. Pooper told the race planners that he would provide portables for, let's say, a thousand dollars; after the races, the event planners would pay him a thousand dollars," she continued.

Dingus added, "But, if *Superpoops* came in with a bid saying they would do it for nine hundred dollars then the race planners would say, 'okay, you win' because that would save them a hundred bucks."

"Go **Superpoops!**" Clayton said, again.

Everyone looked at Clayton. Sometimes Clayton says rather strange things. The portie kids are used to his occasional awkwardness.

"But, **Superpoops** has those old rickety portables and I have heard that half the time they don't even have booty-wipe in them!" said Rhea as she jumped. Rhea was jumping so high she looked like she was flying.

"Are you going to try a triple flip this weekend?" Dingus asked Rhea.

"I've never done one, yet, so I don't know. Are you?" Rhea asked Dingus.

Dingus thought for a second, then said "Do you think your mom would come down and help me?"

"I don't see why not. I will ask her. She's getting ready for the weekend," said Rhea.

Getting ready for an event isn't too hard for porties. They go somewhere almost every weekend. The Portapotty Palace and the rest of the portables stay on the trailer and get taken wherever needed. The portie families just hook up their trucks and go.

When they get to the event, they line up the portables and unhook their trucks.

Just then, Rhea's mom appeared at the trampolines.

"Hi Miss Di" the kids called in unison. The portie kids started showing off a little when Miss Diane appeared.

"Hey, how's everyone doing tonight?" asked Diane.

Rhea told her mom that the kids weren't too happy about missing the school bus figure-eight races this weekend but were excited about the trampolines and the mud.

"You guys are improving so much. I think the portie kids are going to do well in competition this weekend. Anyone need any help with anything?" asked Diane.

Dingus was the first to speak up. "I want to try a triple flip, but I am not sure if I am jumping high enough. I think Rhea will be able to do it easily."

"Dingus, let's see what you've got," Diane said as she jumped up and landed on the wall.

Dingus jumped really high a couple of times and then went straight into his double. He did it perfectly.

"No problem Dingus!" said Diane, "you've totally mastered that double. I am pretty sure you are ready to do a triple. You have plenty of air."

Dingus tried it. It worked! He did a perfect triple! Diane was quite impressed.

"Great Job, Dingus! You have nothing to worry about, just keep practicing like you always do! Rhea, let's see your double flip. Who else wants to try the triple?" Diane asked the others.

Little Lou raised his hand and so did Dump, one of the older boys. Surprisingly, Stinky raised his hand, too.

After Rhea jumped super high, she went straight into a triple flip without doing a double flip! Everyone was shocked and cheering. One of the best things about being a portie kid is that everyone always cheers for each other.

"Wow! You nailed it, Rhea!" Diane smiled proudly for her daughter.

"Okay Lou, are you ready to show me your double flip?" Diane asked Lou. Lou loved hanging out with the bigger kids.

His first attempt at the double wasn't quite there, so he tried it again. The second flip was better, but Diane didn't think he was quite ready to try the triple. She broke it to him gently.

"Lou," she said, "you are doing great for your size. I bet you are the only six-year old around to try a double. You are getting much better. I would like to see you get just a little higher before trying the triple. Keep practicing, okay?"

Lou was a little disappointed that he wasn't able to do the triple flip.

"Hey buddy," said Dingus, "you are the best six-year old tramp trickster in all of the United States, and probably Canada, too!"

Lou felt a little better and smiled up at Dingus.

"You think so? Canada, too?"

Dingus smiled back.

"Canada, too," he assured his little friend.

Next was Stinky's turn to show Diane his double flip. Dingus was surprised that Stinky was showing his double to Miss Diane. Dingus was pretty sure his friend could not jump high enough to do a triple.

"Let's go Stinky!" he shouted anyway.

Dingus watched Stinky jump and jump, and jump some more, until he was jumping pretty high. Then Stinky jumped again a few more times. Miss Diane was just waiting. Everyone was waiting.

"You can do it!" shouted one of the other kids. Finally, Stinky did it. He jumped as high as he possibly could. Then, instead of doing a double, he performed the most beautiful slow motion single flip anyone had ever seen. Surprisingly, while he was bottoms up, Stinky let a fart rip as loudly as he possibly could!

Everyone heard it. They were laughing so hard; some kids were falling on the ground. Ima, Mr. Pooper's fifteen-year-old niece, just stared at Stinky, then busted out laughing too. Her boyfriend, Dump, was cracking up. No one had ever seen that before.

Dingus was laughing the loudest. He immediately jumped on a trampoline and tried to imitate Stinky. So did Clayton Brown and some others. No one could do it like Stinky, though, but they kept trying!

"Okay, boys," said Diane as she rolled her eyes, "are you ready to get serious? We have a Flippin' Mud Festival this weekend? You need to be prepared."

When they all settled down, Dump got on a trampoline and showed his double to Miss Diane.

"You are ready, Dump! Go for it!" she said.

Dump tried but didn't quite make it his first time. Ima pushed the mat under him to break his fall. After a couple of tries, he was able to do a triple and land on his feet. Everyone cheered for him. The kids practiced their forward and backward flips, their kabooms and their codys.

As it started getting dark, everyone headed back to their own portables. When Stinky and Dingus were on their scooters, Dingus asked Stinky how he was able to let that fart fly right at the perfect time?

"I was prepared, and I had confidence!" Stinky said and smiled.

"Prepared?" Dingus questioned.

"I had beans for dinner!"

They both laughed so hard again they almost fell off their scooter. Dingus wondered out loud if Stinky was going to fart at the Flippin' Mud Festival?

"I don't know Dingus, we will have to see!"

CHAPTER 4

CHEAPER IS NOT ALWAYS BETTER

"You get what you pay for."

"That shipment better get here soon, Mr. Swurlee," said Constance Patience. "We have to set up at the school bus figure-eight races by noon tomorrow and the concert by four!"

Constance Patience was the new marketing director for **Superpoops**. Her voice sounded worried while she nervously tapped her pen on the big desk.

It was Friday afternoon and the short, blond woman was impatiently waiting for the truck that was supposed to be delivering three dozen skinny, tall pop-up tents. **Superpoops** was trying out their new pop-up potties at the school bus races this weekend.

Mr. Swurlee, the owner of **Superpoops**, was not worried at all. He was sucking on a cigar and looked as relaxed as he could be. He was also excited. Ever since he came up with this new idea on how to save money on portables, he was on cloud nine. He had just talked to the guy from **Pop-ups** who promised him the skinny, tall tents would arrive in time for tomorrow's events.

"You need to be patient, Constance. They will be here on time."

Constance was worried about Mr. Swurlee's latest get rich quick scheme. "But," she thought to herself, "if Mr. Swurlee gets rich, I get rich, too!" It was a far out plan, but it just might work.

"Now, where is that delivery truck," she muttered to herself while looking at her watch.

"I will be out cutting those noodles," Mr. Swurlee said. He grabbed his root beer and headed toward the garage.

"This is going to be the best money-making weekend in **Superpoops** history!" he laughed. "Oh, if Sandy calls, come out and get me. I need to talk to her."

Sandy Tizer is Mr. Swurlee's niece. Mr. Swurlee is what some may call a cheapskate. He has very few employees. Sandy does most of the work for the portables on the weekends. Actually, her six boys do the work. The Tizer boys go to school with *Pooper's* portie kids. All the Tizer boy's names start with the letter J: Jacob, Jeremy, Jack, Jerry, Josh, and Joe.

Mr. Swurlee likes Sandy's boys because they always do what they are told, they don't say much, and they stay out of sight. He doesn't always know where they are, but if they aren't bothering him, he doesn't care.

The owner of **Superpoops** wears blue and white, striped overalls on most days. With his thick, red hair and red beard, he clomps around in big yellow boots. He looks like a clown that just stepped off a caboose.

Out in the garage, Mr. Swurlee got started on his new money-making venture. In the corner, was a box full of swim noodles. He took each of the colorful noodles, cut them in half, then slit them down the whole length of the noodle. After he slit them, he put them in a different box.

Along the wall of the garage, were stacks of five-gallon pickle buckets. Mr. Swurlee had been collecting pickle buckets for years. Whenever he went to a restaurant, he would ask them if they had any. Most restaurants have extra pickle buckets lying around and were happy to give them to him. He never had any particular use for them. If he needed a seat, he would grab a bucket, turn it upside down, and sit on it. If he needed to carry anything, he would put it in a bucket and tote it around. He just loved his buckets.

One day, while sitting in one of his rickety portables, he saw a picture on Pinterest that made his eyes pop out of his head!

"Yes! Yes! Yes!" he roared with his biggest, deepest, voice. He was so loud that Constance Patience ran out into the yard to see what the matter was!

"Is something wrong, Mr. Swurlee? Are you okay?" she hollered out into the lot.

"Everything is great, and I am great, Constance!" Mr. Swurlee came barreling out of a portable, smiling.

"We are going to be rich, rich! Sit down *Pooper's! Superpoops* is about to be number one!"

What Mr. Swurlee saw on Pinterest was a way to save a lot of money on portable toilets. It was a picture of a five-gallon bucket just like his pickle buckets. Along the rim of the bucket was a pink swim noodle that had been split so it would fit snugly around the rim of the bucket. The swim noodle held a garbage bag in the bucket. The five-gallon bucket was being used as a portable toilet!

"What a great idea!" he thought.

Constance Patience looked at the picture on Mr. Swurlee's phone. Her eyes got wildly excited like her bosses. The two of them started dancing around the lot.

"We're going to be rich! We're going to be rich!" they sang together.

After Mr. Swurlee slit all the swim noodles, he picked up a box of kitchen size garbage bags. He pulled out a garbage bag, opened it up and placed it in a pickle bucket with the edges hanging over the rim. Then, he carefully pushed the noodle onto the rim of the pickle bucket, holding the garbage bag perfectly in place.

He was thrilled to see how easy this was going to be, and cheap! Instead of bringing in his big truck to deliver, pump and clean his big, old, plastic portables, Mr. Swurlee would just have the Tizer boys change the garbage bags in the toilet buckets. The toilet buckets will fit perfectly in the easy pop-up, skinny, tall tents.

No more paying for trucks and trailers to haul and set up the portables. He will have Sandy's boys set up the pop-up tents and put a toilet bucket in each one. The boys can take down the portable tents in a few seconds and the toilet buckets will stack up in the back of Sandy's pickup truck.

Mr. Swurlee thought of almost everything for his new pop-up portable toilet invention. There was one detail he forgot to work out. He had about twenty-four hours to figure that out.

CHAPTER 5

THE SUPER TP SPIT WAD SHOOTER

"TGIF. Thank goodness it's Friday"

The yellow school bus pulled up to *Pooper's Portables*. It was Friday, so the portable toilets were attached to big trucks and lined up like a parade waiting for the portie kids to get home from school. There was The Portapotty Palace, The Pott's Pots, The Johns' Jons, The Brown House and the rest. Everyone was loaded and ready to go to The Flippin' Mud Festival. Each of the kids filed off the bus and jumped into their parent's truck.

"Can Stinky ride with us, Mom?" Dingus asked as he opened the back door.

"If it's okay with Mrs. Johns," Mom replied.

Dingus waved to Stinky.

"Come on, she said yes!" hollered Dingus.

Stinky ran over and climbed into the Slopp's truck. He was carrying two crazy contraptions with toilet paper rolls attached to them. They had a trigger and a water bottle on top.

"What the heck are those?" Mom asked with her eyes looking squinty as she tried to figure out what they were.

"No way!" shouted Dingus. "Oh, my gosh! I have been wanting one of those forever! You got two?"

"One is for you!" Stinky said to his best friend.

Dingus could not believe his eyes. Stinky handed him one of the two Super TP Spit Wad Shooters.

"This is the best day ever!" Dingus shouted.

"Wait Pop!" Dingus said. "We need some water. We gotta have water to make them work."

"No, Dingus! My dad already put water in them for us. They are ready to shoot!" Stinky smiled.

Dingus remembered the first time he saw the Super TP Spit Wad Shooter online. He told Stinky about it and they decided they were both going to ask for one for their birthday.

"Why did your dad buy these for us, Stinky? Our birthdays aren't until August" Dingus asked as he looked through the site on his new toy.

"I don't know, I showed him the video. I guess he liked them too. I can't wait 'til we get to the festival. How long 'til we get there, Mr. Slopp?" Stinky asked from the back seat.

Pop looked at the GPS screen. "Looks like we should be there in about twenty-three minutes, guys."

As the boys were fiddling with their new spit wad shooters, Dingus started thinking about the school bus races they were supposed to be going to this weekend. He pulled lightly on the trigger to see how it worked, he could see that the toilet paper roll turned when he pulled the trigger. Then the toilet paper went through the cutter before it got wet. He thought it was cool and couldn't wait to shoot it.

"Pop, I was wondering about something," said Dingus.

"What's that son?" Pop asked.

"Why did *Pooper's* lose the bid to **Superpoops** for the school bus figure-eight races? We really wanted to go again this year."

"Well, Gus," Pop said as he kept his eyes on the road and his hands on the big steering wheel, "I can't say for sure, but Mr. Swurlee must have offered the event planners a pretty good deal to switch to **Superpoops**. From what I have heard, Mr. Swurlee saves money by having old run-down portables, and he doesn't spend money servicing them either."

Mom chimed in, "And, I heard the specks better bring their own booty-wipe and sanitizer with them if they want it!"

"Apparently, Mr. Swurlee doesn't have a nose because they smell terrible too," added Pop.

"Eeeeew!" said Stinky. "That's bad!"

At the same time Stinky said it, he accidentally pulled the trigger of his spit wad shooter and fired off a spit wad, hitting Mom right on her neck!

"Oh! Stinky!" screamed Mom, "That is nasty!"

Dingus couldn't help but laugh when he saw that splat on mom's neck. Stinky quickly apologized to Mom.

"I am so sorry Mrs. Slopp!" he said, quite embarrassed. His face was red, but he was trying to hold in his laugh at that same time.

Stinky looked over at Dingus to see him laughing. Dingus was trying to laugh as quietly as possible. His head was down in his lap and his arm was over his face so Mom would not see him. Both boys were having a hard time not busting out loud.

"You boys better be careful with those things or you are going to get into trouble!"

said Mom as she reached up and wiped the spit wad off her neck. She was not happy.

"We will, we promise," said Dingus.

"Sorry," said Stinky, again.

"I was thinking," said Pop. "How would you guys like to go to the school bus races tonight?"

The boys looked at each other.

"What? What?" they both said at the same time.

"Yeah, I have been thinking. The school bus figure-eight race starts at seven. We should have the portables set up and ready to go in plenty of time." Pop explained.

"Oh, Pop! That would be awesome! Can we, please?" Dingus shouted a little louder than he expected.

Pop looked over at Mom.

"What do you think, Mom? Would that be okay?"

"I don't know if they can be trusted," Mom said jokingly. "If I get hit by anymore spit wads, these two boys won't be going anywhere for a long, long time!"

"We promise, Mom. We won't shoot anymore spit wads at you. Please, Mom?" Dingus begged.

"I suppose it will be all right," she said with a smile.

"Yes!" Stinky shouted, "We are going to the school bus figure-eight races!"

Dingus couldn't believe the surprise Pop just sprung on them. He didn't know Pop was even thinking about taking them.

"They are just over at the fairgrounds. It shouldn't be too big of a deal. You boys must be on your best behavior, though. If not, you two will both be on extra-cleaning duty for a month straight."

"We will be good, Pop." Dingus said in a serious voice. "You can trust us."

"I hope so. You won't be able to take your spit wad shooter things, you know, right?" Pop reminded them.

"We know," said Stinky. "They won't let us in through security with it, I am pretty sure."

"Yes, exactly," said Pop.

In the backseat, the boys were fist bumping and high fiving.

"We are going to the races!" Dingus said to Stinky in disbelief.

"Unbelievable! Your Pop is the best!" Stinky said.

"I wonder if there will be any crashes tonight?" Dingus said smiling with curiosity.

CHAPTER 6

FRIDAY NIGHT SET UP

"That sounds like good advice!"

As The Portapotty Palace pulled up to The Flippin' Mud Festival, Dingus could see the trampolines had already been placed around the grounds. The excavators were pushing and pulling dirt around as the water trucks were filling the pits to create the mud. Dingus thought making mud pits looked like fun. He started getting excited about tomorrow's events.

Dingus had never been to, nor ever seen, a trampoline mud challenge. He had no idea what to expect. Would he be able to do flips all covered in mud? He wasn't sure.

After the Slopp family set up The Portapotty Palace in the line-up, next to the other porties, Dingus did his daily plunge and clean. As always, after he was finished, he put all the switches back to the center position and closed the valve.

"I'm going to check out the trampolines with everybody," Dingus hollered. Mom was setting up the outdoor kitchen with the other portie parents in the big open area behind the porties.

"Be back here in thirty minutes, Dingus, dinner will be ready," Mom replied.

Dingus headed over to the neon orange trampoline where some other portie kids were gathering. There was a padded wall set up next to it for jumping off and on. Stinky was standing next to Rhea and EvyPoo. A young woman was practicing on the trampoline.

"Do you guys jump?" she asked as she bounced up and down.

The porties looked at each other and smiled.

"We like to mess around on the trampolines a bit. How about you?" Rhea said.

The young woman had a long, dark, braid pulled into a scrunchy. She said she was hoping to get into the finals. Then she did a double flip. She was tight in her flips and landed perfectly on her feet.

"Nice!" said EvyPoo. "Most of us porties are competing tomorrow, but we have never done the mud and trampoline together."

"Let me give you a little advice about the mud," the girl said as she continued jumping. "Don't be afraid to clean up really well in the fountains before getting back on the trampolines." She smiled, then added, "Most newbies try to skip through the fountains too quickly, but you can't. Mud on the tramps will mess up your flips and your kabooms, I promise."

"Thanks!" said Rhea, "appreciate that!"

"You bet!" she continued. "Hey, do you guys know The Frog? He's a vlogger."

"Yeah, of course!" said Dingus. The Frog was Dingus' absolute favorite vlogger.

"I heard he was going to be here tomorrow, so look for him!" Said the jumper.

"No way, that is crazy!" said Stinky. "Dude, we love that guy!"

"Awesome!" exclaimed Dingus.

Suddenly, Dingus remembered they were going to the school bus races tonight! He gave Stinky a friendly hit on the arm like friends sometimes do.

"Hey," he turned toward EvyPoo. "Are you guys going to the school bus races with us? My dad said we get to go!"

"Really? I don't know. I will have to ask my parents." EvyPoo said.

"I want to go!" shouted Lou. He wasn't sure his parents were going to let him stay out so late.

"I am going to go ask my mom right now," the little guy said as he ran off toward the portables. The rest of the portie kids walked around the park to check out the different trampolines. Dingus was trying to figure out how the course was set up. All the kids agreed that the neon trampolines were pretty rad. They were careful to steer clear of the tractors making the mud, but they enjoyed watching them.

After dinner, Pop piled seven of the portie kids, including Lou, into his big truck. Dump decided to go too, offering to keep an eye on Lou.

Clayton came along, although Dingus and Stinky were a little nervous about him coming. It seemed wherever Clayton went, trouble seemed to follow. Tonight was no exception.

CHAPTER 7

SKINNY, TALL TENTS

"If you gotta go, you gotta go!"

Sure enough, as soon as Pop got on the road, Clayton made an announcement.

"Mr. Slopp, I gotta go to the bathroom."

"Really, Clayton?" Pop exclaimed in disbelief. "You didn't think about that before you left The Brown House?"

"I didn't have to go then," Clayton said while shaking his knee up and down as if he had to go very soon, or else!

"The fairgrounds are not too far. We will be there before you know it. You should be able to hold it, buddy."

"Okay," said Clayton.

The line of cars going into the fairgrounds parking lot was winding out to the main road and going fairly slow. Dingus and the others were getting excited about seeing the races.

"Pop, can we get some cotton candy if they have it?" Dingus had a sweet tooth and loved cotton candy. Mom didn't usually let him have it when she was around.

"Gus, you know your mom wouldn't approve," Pop said with a wink in his eye. "If I let you get some, you better not tell her, or I am going to hear about it."

"Deal," said Dingus, smiling.

"I want cotton candy too," said Lou.

"I want to get some popcorn," EvyPoo said to Rhea. "Want to share some?"

"Sure!" Rhea said while looking in her purse. "I forgot to bring any money."

"No problem," EvyPoo replied, "I still have my allowance."

Finally, Pop pulled the truck into a parking spot. It was pretty far from the entry gate because there were so many specks. Clayton jumped out and started running toward the entrance.

"Clayton," yelled Pop. "Do you have money for your ticket?"

"I can't wait, I gotta go!" Clayton yelled back.

Of course, the ticket takers at the gate did not let him go through the gate. Clayton started dancing around like a maniac.

"I gotta go, I gotta go." he kept saying over and over until Pop finally came with the tickets from the ticket booth.

"Here ya go, Clayton," Pop said as he handed the ticket to him. "Excuse me, but where are the portables?" Pop asked the ticket taker.

"They should be over to the left, but I haven't seen the trucks bring 'em in yet," the ticket taker said as he shrugged his shoulders.

"Go to the left, Clayton," Pop said and pointed. Clayton started running.

"I don't see them. They're not here!" Clayton screamed, almost in tears.

"I see some tents, but no portables."

When Dingus and the rest of the porties caught up with Clayton, they saw a line of six, skinny, tall tents facing another row of six, skinny, tall tents.

"Hey, there's a sign," said Dump pointing to a tree.

"It says 'Welcome to *Superpoops* Pop-up Potties'."

"What the heck?" Clayton cried out in disbelief. "Where am I supposed to go to the bathroom? Where are the portables?"

His voice got louder with each sentence.

"Where am I supposed to pee? Where are the Pop-up Potties they are talking about?" He yelled.

Clayton was causing a scene, but no one seemed to mind because everyone wanted to know where the portables were. The portie kids were looking at the skinny, tall tents wondering if possibly, those were the portables. Hanging on the side of each skinny, tall tent was an upside-down bottle of sanitizer.

Pop started laughing as soon as he realized that the skinny, tall tents, were in fact, supposed to be the portables. On the front side of each tent was a flap which served as a door. It must have had some type of hook and loop fastener to keep it closed from the inside.

"What's so funny Mr. Slopp?" Clayton said to Pop.

"Oh, Clayton, I am not laughing at you," said Pop.

He then pulled back the nylon door of the tent, revealing a white, five-gallon pickle bucket with an orange pool noodle around its rim.

"I am laughing because Mr. Swurlee has managed to create the cheapest portables ever!"

When Clayton and the other porties saw the buckets in the tents, they were shocked. They all looked at each other and then at the buckets again.

"No way!" Clayton shouted.

The portie kids cracked up when they realized that *Superpoop's* pop-up potties were just skinny, tall tents with pickle buckets in them.

"I can't pee in a bucket. I've never peed in a bucket before!" The redhead yelled.

"Clayton, Clayton! You will be fine. Come on over here," Pop said as he led Clayton toward the tent. Clayton looked into the strange space. It was rather dark, but he could see his only choice was to pee in the bucket. There was a garbage bag in the bucket, held neatly with the swim noodle. He had to go so badly.

Dingus and Stinky looked in the other tents. They all had noodle rimmed buckets in them. The noodles were all different colors. Some of them had booty-wipe hanging in them and some of them did not. Dangling on the outside of the pop-ups were squirt bottles filled with sanitizer.

Right then, EvyPoo and Rhea decided they were not going to eat or drink anything at the races.

"No way am I using one of those!" said EvyPoo.

"Me, neither!" agreed Rhea.

Dingus and Stinky were thinking the same thing. They were not going to use those silly buckets.

Behind the skinny, tall tents, Dingus saw two of Sandy Tizer's boys sword fighting with some sticks. No one said anything to them. The Tizer boys were not really the friendly type.

When Clayton came out of the skinny, tall tent, he looked very relieved. Then, weirdly, Jack Tizer dropped his stick and walked into the tent Clayton had just walked out. When Jack came out, he looked at his brother, shrugged his shoulders, then went back to sword fighting.

"That was not right," Clayton mumbled.

"Don't forget to use the sanitizer, Clayton," said Pop.

Clayton opened the upside-down bottle and gave it a squeeze. Sanitizer went on his hand and all over his shirt, too.

"Grrrr," Clayton growled.

"Let's get going." Pop said, then added, "Does anyone else need to use a bucket?"

Dingus looked at Stinky and they both started laughing.

"No, we're good," Dingus smiled.

Lou looked up at Dump and said,

"Um… I think I should go. Do I have to go in a bucket, too?"

"I'm afraid so," Dump replied.

After Lou used the bucket, and carefully used the sanitizer, the *Pooper's* gang went up to the spectator stands. The other Tizer boys were sitting on the bottom bleacher by the steps. As the portie kids walked by, the Tizer's snarled at them. Dingus knew the Tizer boys from school but didn't play with them much.

"**Superpoops** is going to take all of your potty business," the oldest Tizer boy, Josh, said to Dingus.

Dingus didn't know what to say so he said nothing and walked on by. Pop led the kids to the top bleachers where they liked to sit.

"Why did those Tizer boys look at us like that?" Asked EvyPoo to Pop.

"I have no idea," said Pop. "I don't think I would be very pleasant if I had to take care of those crazy pop-up portables. What are they going to do with the garbage bags when they are full of waste?"

"Eeeeww!" said EvyPoo.

As soon as Dingus sat down on the cool metal bleacher, he suddenly had the strangest memory pop up in his head. It was a memory from last year's school bus races, when the school bus hit the light pole that fell on the portables. He remembered seeing a boy come running out of The Portapotty Palace so mad because people were hollering at him.

"Get out of the Portables! Get out of the Portables!" they yelled.

The boy was struggling to pull his pants up as the light pole was falling. Dingus just realized that boy was Jerry Tizer!

"Stinky!" shouted Dingus. "Remember last year when the light pole fell on your Jon?" All the kids turned to listen to Dingus.

"Yeah," said Stinky, "how could I forget? I didn't have my own bed for about two weeks when it was getting repaired!"

"I just realized it was Jerry Tizer who came running out of The Portapotty Palace with his pants down. Remember? He was so angry!"

"What? That was Jerry Tizer? Oh yeah!" remembered Stinky.

"I remember!" laughed Dump. "He was trying to get his pants buttoned when he came out!"

"I just saw his face and it hit me; it was him!" said Dingus.

Stinky was cracking up. "Maybe that's why they looked at us like that. They are probably still mad because we were laughing so hard."

"But it was so funny," said Dingus. "Luckily, no one got hurt!"

The school bus figure-eight races were starting soon. The sun was going down. The portie kids were ready for some fun.

Dingus kept thinking about those crazy skinny, tall tents and pickle buckets. What in the world did they plan to do with the garbage bags when they were filled with waste? He nudged Stinky to get his attention.

"I still can't believe *Superpoops* is using those cheap pop-up potties!" Dingus said. "No wonder they won the bid for this event! *Pooper's Portables* has been in business for forty-five years. We can't let those Tizer boys run us out of town with some cheap tents, pickle buckets, and swim noodles!"

"The school bus race is our event!" Stinky proclaimed. "We have been bringing our portables to the school bus races our whole life!"

When Dingus and Stinky started talking about *Superpoops* taking *Pooper's Portables* business they started getting upset. They loved Mr. Pooper and the whole *Pooper's Portable* family.

"We can't let *Superpoops* take *Pooper's* business! We've gotta do something!" Stinky said to Dingus.

"You are right. Pooper's has always been number one in the portables business," replied Dingus.

"We won't stand for number two!" The curly-haired boy said with a look of determination in his eye.

"We've gotta do something."

CHAPTER 8

THE RACES

"The wheels on the bus go 'round and 'round."

There was a huge attendance at the racetrack. Specks love the school bus figure-eight races. Although the sun was going down, it was still pretty warm. The crowd was settling into their seats.

All the specks were eating hot dogs, popcorn, and cotton candy. Even though the racetrack was giving away special drink cups that had pictures of the school buses on them, the portie kids all said "no thank you!" to a drink. Pooper's porties were not going to use Superpoop's pop-up potties if they didn't absolutely have to use them.

"Garbage bags? Really?" said Dingus again in disbelief.

"That is nasty," said EvyPoo to Dingus. "I guess they will change the bags when they get filled up. I wonder where they are putting them?"

The school buses were lining up to start the figure-eight races soon. The announcer announced the names of the buses. All of the portie's favorite buses were there including Big Banana, Bumble Bee, the Yellow Yeti, the Lemon Limo, and the Blue Bomber. Dingus saw the Yellow Submarine was there, too.

"Look, on the front bumper!" said Dingus to Stinky as he pointed, "That's where the Yellow Submarine ran into the pole!"

"I wonder if there will be anything exciting like that this year," said Stinky.

"Let's hope not, boys," said Pop in his fatherly voice. "We don't need any accidents this year."

Some of the portie kids were standing up on the top bleachers watching the buses line up. The drivers liked going in and out of their buses and having fun with the specks. The announcer called some speck kids to come down and meet the drivers. The portie kids were hoping they would be called down. Unfortunately, none of them heard their name. They were okay with it, though. Last year, three of them were called down to play games and win prizes.

Clayton was not watching the track. He was standing up looking over the back of the bleachers. He could see the pop-up potties and the line of people needing to use them. Clayton saw some people plugging their noses.

"I can see the potty tents from here." Clayton announced.

Dingus turned around to see what was going on. He saw the Tizer boys throwing the white garbage bags onto the road behind the tents. The garbage bags looked like marshmallows from the top of the bleachers.

The Tizer's were taking turns going into the pop-up portables to check the pickle buckets. Whenever a bag in a bucket got full, one Tizer boy would lift off the noodle, take the bag out of the bucket, tie it up, and put it out in the driveway. The other one would put a new bag in and slip the noodle back over the rim to hold the bag tightly. Then it was ready for the next speck.

"Jack," Josh Tizer said, as he rubbed his nose with the back of his hand. "Do you smell something?"

"Um, yeah, it smells kind of like a barnyard," said Jack.

"But, we're not near any farms." his brother said.

"I think it's our pile of bags. People are plugging their noses. I guess Mr. Swurlee didn't think about these bags smelling so badly." said Jack.

"We need a fan," suggested Josh.

"Where are we going to get a fan?" Jack wondered.

"Jake can go get one from the house," Josh replied. "I'll go ask him."

When Josh took off to find his brother, Jack could hear the crowd getting excited. The races were about to begin. Jack went over and stood by the stands to watch what he could see from there. It wasn't the best view, but he could see some of the buses.

Josh and Jake came back carrying a battery-operated fan with a misting button that Jake found in his backpack.

"Um, I don't really think that is going to help, Jake. It's too small and this stink is getting pretty big!" said Jack.

"Uh, yeah, I guess you're right," said Jake.

"You guys need to go home and get a regular fan," directed Jack, looking seriously.

As Josh and Jake headed out to the parking lot, they walked by the racetrack office. The door to the office was propped open with a big industrial fan blowing at a man sitting at his desk. The man rubbed his nose as the Tizer boys walked by.

Jake had an idea. He walked up to the door of the office and stood next to the big fan.

"Hello," said Jake.

The man looked up from his desk.

"May I help you?" he asked Jake.

"I was wondering if you had another fan that we could borrow. I guess people are complaining about the smell coming from the portables. We need a fan to blow the smell away from the people."

"Is that what I am smelling? What the heck is going on over there? Do the portables need emptying already? The races just started." The man was not happy.

"The pop-up portables that we brought are not the same as regular portables. We are emptying them, a lot. That's the problem," Jake spoke up. "We have to change the bags after every couple of specks."

"Specks go a lot!" chimed in Josh.

"What?" The man did not understand. "What are you talking about? Changing bags?"

"I could go into the details, or you could loan me your fan to try and take care of the smell. May I?" Jake asked as he put his hand on the big handle of the power blower.

"Just take it. Anything to get rid of that smell!" the man exclaimed.

Josh unplugged the big fan and grabbed the orange extension cord wrapping it loosely. Jake carried the fan and the two boys headed back over to the portie area. Jake put the powerful fan right in the middle of the entrance near the sign, hoping the smell would blow away from the specks. The boys found an electrical outlet on the same light pole the school bus hit last year. Luckily, it was fixed, so Josh plugged in the fan.

Unfortunately, as soon as the big fan was plugged in, the Tizer boys realized it was too much wind power. Every one of the skinny, tall tents blew sideways like a hurricane going through. Luckily, the partly full buckets were heavy enough to keep the tents from blowing over completely.

"Unplug it! Unplug it!" Jack yelled.

Josh unplugged it the nick of time. Another minute and the pop-up portables would have been blown right over, buckets and all. What a terrible mess that would have been!

"Holy tornado!" said Jack. "Where on earth did you get that giant fan?"

"The guy in the office was using it. He said we could use it, if it would get rid of the smell."

"Well, that's not going to work either!" exclaimed Jack.

"Jake, listen to me! You have to go home and get our fan! We have to get rid of the smell. The specks are getting really mad! Mr. Swurlee is going to be even madder if the racetrack refuses to pay him because of this big stink!"

"All right," said Jack, reluctantly.

Jack finally went home which was just a few miles from the track and got the regular square fan. It fit perfectly at the end of the pop-up potties. Jack plugged it in and put some flowerpots around it to help with the smell. It helped a little.

The school bus figure-eight races were almost finished and nothing particularly bad happened. There were a lot of close calls. Every year, the Yellow Submarine likes to cause problems and this year was no exception.

In the middle of the race, the big yellow bus just stopped dead center in the middle of the eight!

Every time a bus came around the bottom of the curve, they had to swerve to go around it. Horns were honking and dust was flying. No crashes this year, only near misses on every lap.

Dingus and all of the portie kids loved the excitement of the races. They were also keeping an eye on the action behind them in the pop-up potties. They saw the bags of waste piling up in the driveway. The pile was growing.

So was the smell.

"Where is that smell coming from?" asked Pop. He looked over at Clayton.

"Did you fill your pants?" he asked curiously. Pop would feel bad for any of the portie kids if they pooped their pants.

"That's not me, Mr. Slopp! It's the bags of poop down there!" he said as he pointed down behind the bleachers.

Pop looked down and saw the pile of white garbage bags so high that the Tizer boys could barely throw them on top.

"I'm still wondering what Mr. Swurlee plans on doing with all those bags?" Pop said, shaking his head. "I can't even imagine!"

No, he could not have imagined, in a million years, what was about to happen.

CHAPTER 9

THE SMELLY EXIT

"Say goodbye, Superpoops!"

Dingus and the rest of the portie kids were thrilled that The Blue Bomber won the school bus figure-eight race. Big Banana took a close second and Green Griffin took third. The winners stood on the podium to accept their awards. As they stood on the first, second, and third place risers, Dingus could see them plugging their noses. The man from the office, who was the manager of the racetrack, was also plugging his nose as he congratulated the winners and gave them their trophies. Dingus could see the manager was not happy about the smell coming from the pop-up potties.

As soon as he finished handing out the trophies, the angry man marched straight toward the pop-up potties to talk to the Superpoops kids. He saw the pile of tied up bags and noticed the big power blower was not plugged into the outlet. He looked like he was getting madder with every step he took towards the pile. Still holding his nose, he bent over and plugged the big fan into the outlet. Immediately, it started blowing like a hurricane.

Unfortunately, the boys had moved the fan behind the portables and now it was pointing straight at the pile of garbage bags. As the fierce wind blew across the pile, the smelly bags looked like bubbling marshmallows, not the good kind you see at a campfire!

The drivers went back to their buses, holding up their awards and showing off a bit. They all cruised one more lap around the track so the fans could cheer for their favorite buses. They lined up in the order they finished the race. The Blue Bomber led the cruise.

Up in the stands, the porties were celebrating the Blue Bomber's win. They were screaming, hooting and hollering. Pop did his super loud, finger whistle that just about blew Dingus' eardrums out.

"Say goodbye to our school buses! See you next year!" shouted the announcer.

The buses honked their horns. They opened and shut their doors for their fans as they paraded down the exit drive. They were going pretty fast, too. The drivers loved showing off for the fans.

As the exit gates opened, the school buses drove toward the back driveway. From up top, Dingus and the others had a great view as they left. The porties could see what was going to happen to those bags of waste! It was not going to be pretty!

The buses aimed straight toward the heap of bubbling, stinking, garbage bags! One by one, the buses drove over the white plastic stink bombs. As the tires rolled over the bags, each one popped and exploded! Brown and yellow slime shot out from the bags. It looked like brown oozy swords going in all different directions.

Boom! Pop! Splat! Boom! Splat!
The giant fan didn't help. Instead, it sent the crappy contents all over everything. As the bags exploded, muck burst through the air like confetti. It reminded Dingus of one time when his mom made frosting with her electric mixer. She pulled the spinning blades out of the bowl before turning it off! Frosting flew all over the kitchen.

The stench of the mess was very intense. Specks started screaming. They held their noses and pushed their way out of the stands as quickly as possible. They couldn't get to their cars fast enough.

"Oh, my gosh Stinky! It smells like the nastiest outhouse ever!" hollered Dingus.

"I wish I had my respirator mask right now!" added Stinky.

The girls and Lou were gagging. Dingus, Dump, and Stinky thought it was pretty funny. They were laughing, until they started gagging.

For some reason unknown to anyone, Clayton Brown just sat there plugging his nose and whistling. A lot of times Clayton does things that no one really understands.

The buses slowed down a little, but there was nowhere for them to turn around. They just kept barreling through the mire. Each bus looked so disgusting, dripping with yuck, especially The Blue Bomber!

"It's not the Blue Bomber anymore!" Yelled Stinky. "It's the Brown Bomber!"

Dingus and the others laughed. Even through the smell, it was still funny. Most of the specks had left, but Pooper's porties hung around the top bleachers to see what was going to happen next.

Jack, Jake and Josh Tizer just about lost it when they saw the buses go through the bags. The racetrack manager came running over to the pop-up potties as fast as his tired body could move.

"What in the world is going…," he stopped in the middle of his sentence when he saw what was going on.

"You boys have created the biggest mess in the history of man!" he screamed at the top of his lungs. He was plugging his nose, so it sounded kind of funny. "This needs to be cleaned up immediately! And let Mr. Swurlee and Constance Patience know that Superpoops will never work in this state again if I have anything to say about it!"

"Pop!" Dingus shouted, "Did you hear that?"

Dingus and the other portie kids looked at Dad, then at each other. They all smiled.

"I was pretty sure something crazy was going to happen when I saw those pop-up portables. I just didn't think it was going to be so disastrous for Superpoops and so good for Pooper's!" Pop laughed.

The other Tizer boys gathered down at the mess. It looked like Jake was on his phone, probably talking to Mr. Swurlee. Dingus figured he was telling their boss how well his pop-up potties did NOT work out.

Dingus wondered how they were going to clean up that horrible mess. The drivers parked their disgusting buses in the road outside of the gate.

Out of nowhere, a firetruck pulled up and two big firemen jumped out. They pulled off a hose and hooked it up to the fire hydrant on the corner. One by one, they gave each of the buses a much-needed power wash! The drivers honked their horns in delight. The firemen cleaned up the buses, but they didn't clean up the Tizer's mess.

The racetrack manager appeared with a front-end loader. He scooped up the pile of busted, slimy, garbage bags and plopped them into a nearby dumpster. Unfortunately, the putrid smell lingered.

The Tizer boys watched in disbelief as the manager then scooped up every one of Superpoop's pop-up potties, toilet buckets and all. He dumped every one of Mr. Swurlee's cheap portables straight in the dumpster. The manager had a big smile on his face as he drove away. The only things left in the portie area were the fans and the flowerpots.

Pop finally led Pooper's portie kids down the bleachers and headed toward his big truck.

"I guess we don't have to worry about Superpoops anymore," said Dingus.

"And we didn't have to do anything but watch!" said Stinky.

Both boys were still laughing as they passed the Tizer boys.

"Are you guys coming to The Flippin' Mud Festival tomorrow?" Dingus asked the boys.

"It might not be as fun as this," Stinky added. "But we will definitely have better portables if you need to use one!"

Jake Tizer was so mad about the entire event, he just wanted to punch Stinky for that comment. But, when Jake saw Pop, he stepped back. He looked Stinky straight in the eye instead.

"Oh, we are going to be there all right," he said, "and you can be sure, we will be in your portables!"

"Bet," said Stinky, with a smile.

CHAPTER 10

THE FLIPPIN' MUD COURSE

"Show your colors!"

"Let's go 'Bone Crusher!" Dingus said aloud as he turned the crank on the Mega Power plunger. He was just about done with his daily routine cleaning of The Portapotty Palace. As always, he set the switches back to the center position, closed the valve and waited for the blue deodorized water to fill in the bowls.

After the plunge and clean was done, Dingus got his special lock. It prevents specks from accidentally turning the dial on the door to blue which accesses the lower level. Most specks don't even know about the lower level, so it isn't too big of a deal. With the Portapotty Palace all set, Dingus

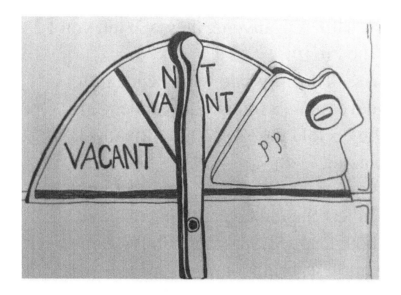

headed over to sign up for The Flippin' Mud Festival.

As he approached the registration table, Dingus saw him, Spence "The Frog" Franklin. The Frog, dressed in a fluorescent green race tee shirt, was signing autographs for some of the judges and volunteers. Dingus ran back to The Portapotty Palace to get his Frog hat that he bought off The Frog's march page.

His hat was in the lower level, sitting on the ping pong table next to his Super TP Spit Wad Shooter. He was so excited to get his hat autographed by The Frog that he forgot to put the special lock back on The Portapotty Palace. He ran back to the registration table as quickly as possible.

"Thanks a lot!" Dingus said after The Frog signed his hat. "Ask anyone, they will tell you I stan' for the Frog!"

"Thanks," The Frog said with a wide grin.

"I've never done a trampoline challenge in mud." Dingus told the Frog. "I don't know how well I'm going to do."

"Don't worry about it, bro," said The Frog "I haven't either! Should be pretty interesting!"

They both laughed. Just then, Stinky came over carrying his new, bright orange, race tee-shirt.

"Have you seen the courses?" Stinky shouted. "They are amazing! You jump from the trampolines straight into the mud!"

"Oh, my gosh! I can't wait to see, now that it's done. I still have to register." said Dingus. "What color do you start in?" Dingus asked.

"I'm at ten-ten orange. I hope you get the same as me!" answered Stinky. Dingus was thinking the same thing.

Unfortunately, when Dingus came back, he had a fluorescent green tee shirt in his hand. That meant Dingus would be starting on the green course. All of the participants received the same color drawstring backpacks for stashing their shirts and shoes when they were jumping.

"I'm twelve o'clock, same as The Frog, can you believe it?" Dingus was so excited. "Did I tell you he autographed my hat!" he added.

"No way, that's lit!" said Stinky, happy for his friend.

Stinky and Dingus changed into their new shirts. As they were leaving, they saw all six of the Tizer brothers heading into the registration area. Dingus and Stinky were surprised to see them.

"Did you know the Tizer's were jumpers?" Dingus asked Stinky.

"I had no idea!" Stinky said, sounding a little perplexed.

"Let's go check out the course," Dingus said. Straight across from the portables was the entrance to the orange course. To the right was the yellow course and to the left, was the green course.

Each course was the same except its color. Each course had three trampolines with one giant mud pit in the middle. One trampoline had a wall next to it for wall tricks. The trampolines only had springs on three sides. The fourth side led straight into the mud pit.

"They're like trampoline diving boards!" Dingus exclaimed.

"That's going to be intense! I have never jumped into a mud pit before!" said Stinky.

"All I know is…you better land on your feet! Can you imagine going head-first into that!" Dingus replied.

"I can't wait!" said Stinky. "This is going to be the best event ever!"

"And look at the fountains, Dingus!" Stinky shouted as he pointed.

"They're like the huge water falls at mini-golf! We get to jump in them! That's crazy!" said Dingus.

"It looks like ten people could stand under the waterfall at one time!" Stinky exclaimed.

Each course had a set of bleachers for specks. Next to the bleachers was a loft that had a table and three chairs on it for the judges. Each judge had a scoring table tent. They were supposed to flip the numbers to reveal their scores.

Dingus had never been judged for his trampoline tricks before. He wondered how he was going to do. Everyone told him he was good. He hoped the judges thought so, too.

A crowd was starting to gather at the registration table. The jumpers were picking up their numbers, tee shirts, backpacks, and schedules. Everyone had to successfully complete the yellow, orange, and green courses before they qualified for the finals.

Just then Stinky felt his breakfast sausage in his stomach.

"Oh no," he said to Dingus. "I don't think I should have eaten sausage for breakfast!"

Suddenly Stinky's voice changed.

"Look over there, Dingus," he said as he pointed to the judges' loft on the orange course.

"What?" Dingus said as he turned to look.

"It's Jerry Tizer and the little one, Joe. They are on the judges loft over there. What the heck are they doing up there?" Stinky wondered aloud.

Dingus looked toward the orange course. The Tizer's were wearing bright yellow shirts, they were easy to spot. Instead of the matching drawstring backpacks, though, they were wearing regular hiking backpacks. Their backpacks were stuffed and bulging.

"They're checking out our portables. Maybe they have diarrhea and want to know where to run in case they have to go in a hurry," said Stinky sarcastically.

"I don't know what those Tizer boys are up to. They were not happy last night!" said Dingus.

"I wonder what they are carrying in those bags, snorkels for the mud?" Stinky laughed.

Dingus and Stinky would have been quite shocked at what was in the boys bulging backpacks. The Tizer boys were not happy about last night's smelly disaster. They also did not like the comments from *Pooper's* porties either. After they got home from their very rough day on the job, they came up with a plan to create a little portable toilet trouble for the *Pooper's* porties at the festival.

Just then, Dingus and Stinky saw some other porties coming toward them.

"Hey Rhea," called Dingus when he saw the girls coming toward them. Rhea was wearing a green shirt and EvyPoo was in orange.

"What time are you starting? I see you are green like me!" Dingus said to Rhea.

"I am at twelve and Evy is at ten-ten" Rhea sounded glad. "What time are you?" She asked.

"I'm twelve also, Stinky is at ten-ten." Dingus said.

"Lou is orange, and at ten-ten too," said Rhea. "We will be able to watch them."

"Oh, that's cool," Dingus said. Then he noticed something wasn't right with Clayton.

"Clayton, man, where's your race shirt and your number?" Clayton just put two fingers on his chin and looked at Dingus trying to think of an answer. When he didn't answer, Dingus shook his head and looked over at Dump. "What about you Dump, what time are you jumping?" he asked his friend.

"I am at twelve, too." Dump said. He was wearing a green shirt.

"Dump," said Dingus, "Did you see the Tizer boys are all here? They seemed pretty mad last night."

Dump was about to give his opinion when three of the Tizer boys appeared around the fountain.

"What's going on, Jake?" Dingus asked nervously.

"*Superpoops* is not going down to *Pooper's Portables*." Jake said looking very serious as his brothers nodded in agreement.

"What do you mean?" Dingus asked, he could tell Jake was pretty mad.

"I am just saying, you better keep an eye on your portables today, that's all," said Jake before turning to his brothers.

"Come on guys, let's get out of here."

As the Tizer's turned around to leave, the porties noticed all of them were wearing big, overstuffed backpacks.

"I wonder what's in their backpacks?" Dingus questioned one more time.

CHAPTER 11

THE TEN-TEN FLIPS

"CRISIS AVERTED!"

"Pop!" Dingus shouted as he approached the picnic tables behind the portables.

"What's up Gus?" said Pop, who was drinking his morning coffee.

"There is something going on with the Tizer boys." Dingus explained what Jake Tizer said.

"Hmmm…" said Pop. "Okay, I will let the other portie parents know. Don't worry about it. You guys go and have fun today. The courses look pretty awesome. I hope you do well today, son."

"Me too, Pop! Did you see it? Even the fountains look rad! See ya," Dingus replied excitedly.

As Dingus headed back, he noticed a slightly unusual smell around the portables. He wasn't too worried about it because he was so excited about The Flippin'" Mud challenge.

Pop made a quick look around the portables, but he did not see anything unusual. He let the other portie parents know what Dingus reported. The line to the portables was short and constant, just like it was supposed to be at this type of event.

"All good there," thought Pop.

He noticed the blue deodorizer smelled a little different, though. It smelled kind of peanut-y. Pop figured someone must have had a peanut butter sandwich nearby. It did not concern him.

Now, if Pop had come over about ten minutes earlier, he would have seen little Joey Tizer standing on his brother Jeremy's shoulders. Little Joe was, in fact, eating a peanut butter sandwich. But, the six-year-old did not like his peanut butter sandwich. He did not like any of the TEN peanut butter sandwiches that his brothers kept handing him. So, while he was up on his brother's shoulders, he stuck the peanut butter sandwiches into the little pipe vents in the tops of *Pooper's* portables.

Pipe vents prevent the build-up of gas and odors in the portables. A clean vent is key to a pleasant toileting experience. *Pooper's Portables* prides itself on providing the best experience possible, including the freshest, deodorized smell.

While Pop was checking around the portables, Dingus went looking for the other porties on the orange course. Stinky, EvyPoo, and Lou were already in the entrance line because it was getting close to their start time. Dump and Rhea were in the bleachers.

Dingus was walking toward the bleachers when he saw Jeremy and Josh Tizer kneeling behind the orange fountain. They were pulling something out of their backpacks. From what Dingus could see, it looked like they had potato shooters, just like the ones at the pumpkin farm they go to every year. Dingus was curious and moved closer in their direction. He couldn't tell what else was in their bags, but he could tell they had something else stuffed in them.

Suddenly Dingus felt a twinge of nervousness in his gut. At the same time, Stinky, who was in line to go up for his first trampoline trick, felt a twinge in his gut. His was not nervousness, though. He came running over to his friend.

"Dingus!" Stinky said urgently. "That sausage is going through me! I gotta go to my portable! Like, now! I can't risk any accidents during my flips," said Stinky.

"I'm going with you. I gotta tell you something," said Dingus. He had to walk quickly to keep up with Stinky.

"What's up?" Stinky asked.

"I saw what Jeremy and Josh Tizer were carrying in their backpacks. You will never guess!" Dingus said.

"What?" said Stinky.

"Potato shooters! That's what!"

"That's messed up, why do they have potato shooters?" Stinky said, certain that Dingus was talking smack.

"I have no idea why! But they do!" Dingus said emphatically.

When Stinky went into his portable to relieve the sausage cramp in his gut, Dingus went into The Portapotty Palace. As he was going in, he noticed that same unusual peanut smell again. He also noticed that the smell of deodorizer and waste was getting stronger. It made him think of the Tizer boys.

"Hey, grab your spit wad shooter, I'm getting mine!" Dingus suggested before he turned his door handle to blue and slid down to the lower level of his portable.

Dingus grabbed his Super TP Spit Wad Shooter that was sitting next to his special lock on the ping pong table where he left it.

"Oh, shoot! I forgot to place my lock," he said to himself. Dingus had a weird feeling somebody had been in his portable but didn't have time to look around. As he was leaving this time, he remembered to place the lock.

If Dingus had taken a better look around The Portapotty Palace, he would have seen Jack Tizer hiding on the other side of his gaming TV!

Because, along with stuffing peanut butter sandwiches into the vent pipes of the portables, the Tizer brothers thought it would be really funny if they flipped the switches on the portables in the wrong direction, to see what would happen. They flipped them in such a way that stuff would go in, that was supposed to go out, and stuff would go up, that was supposed to go down.

As Jack Tizer was flipping the switches on The Portapotty Palace, he noticed the special lock on Dingus' door was missing! Jack tried turning the door handle past the red and into the blue. It worked! It opened right up! There was Dingus' slide that went down to his lower level. Jack had never been in a *Pooper's* Portable. He thought The Portapotty Palace was pretty sweet.

The first thing Jack spotted was the Super TP Spit Wad Shooter sitting on Dingus' ping pong table. He tried it out and thought it was the bomb. In fact, if Dingus would have looked closely at his football team picture, he would have seen that Jack had pretty good aim. There were spit wads sitting square in the faces of Dingus and Stinky!

When Jack overheard Dingus talking to Stinky outside, he grabbed his overstuffed backpack and stuck it behind Dingus' school backpack, then hid beside the giant gaming unit. It had every system imaginable in it. Luckily, Jack was rather thin, so Dingus didn't see him when he came down.

After Dingus left, Jack let out a big sigh of relief, grabbed his backpack, and went to leave The Portapotty Palace. Unfortunately, Jack was not able to get the door open. When the blue lock is on the door, it prevents any lower level access, coming or going.

The young Tizer tried banging on the plastic walls but didn't get any response. Jack wasn't sure what he should do. Because the vents were plugged up, the smell of waste and deodorizer was getting worse and worse. He put on Dingus' deep cleaning respirator mask that was on the shelf. It looked like a bumblebee's face with big round eyes and round filters on the cheeks.

Jack sat down on a gaming chair and decided to load his potato shooter. Instead of potatoes, though, the Tizer's had rolls of toilet paper. So, technically, they had booty-wipe shooters. Jack had eight rolls of booty-wipe stuffed into his backpack. He managed to pack four rolls into the shooter. He was ready for battle, if only he could get himself out of The Portapotty Palace. To take his mind off the impending mess this portable was about to face because of those peanut butter sandwiches his brother crammed into its vent, Jack grabbed the gaming controls and put a game in Dingus' system. It was weird to play games with a mask on. It was weird to be playing someone else's game, too. Luckily for Jack, it was one of his favorite games.

While Jack Tizer was playing games in The Portapotty Palace, Dingus and the other portie kids were back at the orange course.

"It was the best!" Stinky yelled as he came running into the bleachers.

"How did you get dry so fast?" asked Dingus.

"That was the best part! When you come out of the fountain, you walk through this arch thing. It looks like a metal detector, but really, it's a dryer like they have at the carwash! It's a fierce wind tunnel! Straight up, lava!" Stinky had the biggest grin as he was telling Dingus.

The participants had to perform one trick on each trampoline in each color. The judges all watched the same contestant at the same time and revealed their scores immediately after the jump.

"Nice job, Stinky!" Dingus said. "Twenty-seven is great! Did you see Jade "the jumping jelly bean" was in your heat? She slayed it!"

"I think she had a twenty-nine!" said Rhea. "Did you see EvyPoo?" Rhea asked Stinky. "She was on the trampoline next to you, the one with the wall? She did amazing!"

Stinky looked around.

"She was coming up right behind me, I don't know where she went! Lou was right behind me, too." said Stinky

"What was it like to jump in the mud?" asked Dingus.

"It was insane! It was like thin quicksand that only went up to your waist. It was so cool! You are going to love it, Dingus. We should ask Mr. Pooper to put in a mud pit next to our trampoline."

"How did you know what trick to perform?" asked Rhea.

"The volunteer in the line tells you what to do. It's really easy," Stinky explained.

"Next, you go to the green course, then the yellow, right?" asked Dingus.

"Yup," said Stinky.

"Hey, awesome job! You guys did great!" said Dingus as he gave EvyPoo and Lou a high five when they came up the bleachers.

"Stinky, dude! You did it! We could hear your air biscuit all the way over here! Way to go!" Dingus said laughing.

"Strong work, bro!" Dump said. "Do you think the judges gave you extra points for it?" Dump was cracking up.

"You know they did! They couldn't help but laugh, I placed it perfectly on my flip!" laughed Stinky.

"Did you see any of the Tizer's?" asked Rhea.

"I saw a few of them hanging around the fountain area. They are acting weird!" said Stinky.

Dingus looked over toward the fountains. He saw some of the portie parents mulling around at the portables. The strong smell of the portables was spreading over toward the bleachers. This was quite unusual for *Pooper's Portables*.

"What the heck? How come the portables are smelling so badly today?" Dingus exclaimed. "Stinky, have you been practicing your butt blasters everywhere?"

They all laughed, especially Stinky.

"I hope everything is okay with the portables" said EvyPoo. "The parents will figure it out."

"I hope they figure it out soon! Come on, we gotta get over to the green course!" Stinky said to EvyPoo and Lou. The three of them took off.

Dingus carried both of the Super TP Spit Wad Shooters as he, Dump and Rhea walked over to the green bleachers. That's when they realized Clayton was missing, again.

"Where is that kid?" Dump wondered out loud.

The portie parents were inspecting the portables thoroughly at this point. They could certainly tell something was wrong. The smell was getting bad. They were checking all the portables, inside and out. That's when Pop found Jack Tizer playing video games down in Dingus' lower level.

"Hello Mr. Slopp!" said Jack nervously, as he quickly jumped up and took Dingus' mask off his head. "I got trapped down here and couldn't get out." That's all Jack said as he gathered up his stuff and ran past Pop before any questions were asked.

Pop was surprised to see Jack Tizer. He looked around Dingus' game room but didn't see any problems. He shrugged his shoulders and continued looking for the cause of the stench.

The portie parents decided to do a quick power plunge on their portables to see if that would help get rid of the smell. Pop hung up a temporary "CLOSED" sign then put on his personal protective equipment. He went around to the back of The Portapotty Palace. That's when he noticed the switches that Jack had flipped the wrong way.

Pop knew Dingus never left the switches in the wrong position. He immediately suspected the Tizer boys. Dingus had told Pop he thought they might be plotting some kind of prank. Luckily, Pop found the flipped switches before any major mishap took place at The Portapotty Palace. It could have been very messy.

Pop told the other portie parents to check their switches.

Stinky's dad, Mr. Johns looked at his.

"Mine are messed up!" he hollered.

"How about yours, Di?" Pop asked Rhea's mom.

Diane looked at her switches.

"Oh, my gosh yes!" exclaimed Diane.

"Ours too!" said EvyPoo's dad.

Everyone's switches were flipped in the wrong direction!

"Thank goodness we figured this out before anyone cranked their power plunger! Can you imagine what could have happened?" asked Pop, a little freaked out by the thought.

The portie parents all stood in their masks and gloves feeling very relieved that nothing bad happened to their portables. *Pooper's* porties were proud of their business and did not wish anything to happen that might give *Pooper's* a dirty reputation.

The porties were happy the Tizer boy's prank was an epic fail. They obviously had no idea about prank number two.

CHAPTER 12

PRANK NUMBER TWO

"We found the smell"

Unfortunately, the porties relief quickly turned into disbelief! A very strange thing happened next. *Pooper's* beloved portables suddenly started making weird, creaking noises. The plastic buildings seemed to be getting active, if that were possible. The smell was getting unbearable, too.

Everyone in the park started noticing the bizarre shaking of the portables. The specks who were waiting in line for Pop to take the "CLOSED" sign down, stared with anticipation. No one had ever seen portables shake and shiver. What was happening?

As Stinky, EvyPoo, and Lou were in line to perform their trampoline tricks at the green course, the other portie kids came down from the bleachers to see what was happening with the portables.

"What's going on?" asked Dingus, as they all stood bewildered.

"Get back!" yelled Pop to Dingus and the others. He put his arms out wide. Pop had seen something like this years ago when he was a portie kid. A squirrel had piled a bunch of nuts in the pipe vent of one of their portables. He remembered it vividly. The gas vapors were unable to escape, causing the portable to explode!

Right after Pop yelled at the kids to get back, it happened! The pressure in the portables was too much. The portables literally erupted!

Dingus couldn't believe his eyes. First, something shot out of the pipe vents, straight into the sky.

Then, "GULL-LURP" went the blue water. It sounded like the portables were releasing giant burps. No one had ever heard a portable burp before. They braced themselves for whatever might happen next.

Then, nearly a dozen underwater explosions happened all at once. The doors of the portable burst open and toilet paper rolls shot out like giant popcorn kernels coming out of big, colorful poppers. The explosion caused the staircases to flip down and the floors leading to the lower levels to burst open, even the ones that were locked! The pressure caused a few of the portables to actually tip and fall over on the next ones. Luckily, The Portapotty Palace was on the end. It was stable and bore the weight of the John's Jon which was leaning against it.

The specks and the porties could not believe their eyes! What on earth could have caused such an event they wondered? Mr. **Pooper's** *Portables* had never done anything like that before.

When the peanut butter sandwiches that Little Joe Tizer stuffed into the pipe vents started falling from the sky, the answer became clear.

Dingus looked around at everyone watching the portables. There were no Tizer boys in sight. He saw Stinky, EvyPoo, and Lou. They were coming over to the portables after performing on the green course.

"What happened? What's going on?" Stinky saw the mess created by the portables.

"The portables exploded!" Dingus told him. "Someone plugged up the pipe vents with peanut butter sandwiches and they all exploded!"

"Did anyone see the Tizer boys around here?" Pop asked.

"Last time I saw them, they were over by the yellow fountains," said Dump.

Pop and the other porties quickly tried to put the portables back in order. The women stashed ladders and closed doors. The men put the tipped portables back upright and made sure they were level. The kids picked up the toilet paper rolls from the lawn and straightened up the portables.

Dingus had a lot of straightening to do in his lower level. That's when he saw the spit wads on his football picture. Only a Tizer would shoot spit wads at his picture or jam up the pipes to cause an explosion. It was clear the Tizer boys wanted to ruin Pooper's Portable's and put them out of business.

Dingus saw it was eleven fifteen. He needed to start thinking about going over to the green course to do his first trick, but he couldn't get the sound of

the portables burping, or the spit wads on his picture, out of his mind.

Dingus wanted to see Stinky, EvyPoo, and Lou perform on the yellow course. While he was walking toward it, he kept his eyes out for the Tizer boys. Hopefully they didn't have any more pranks up their sleeves. Exploding portables was enough for one day!

He got to the yellow course just in time to see Stinky doing this first trick. It was a kaboom. Stinky was really good at his backward rotation. A kaboom is not easy and requires a lot of practice. Stinky did it great. After the kaboom, he forward flipped, then farted, before landing in the mud. Dingus thought Stinky might make it into the finals with that trick, if the judges were not offended by the fart, of course!

EvyPoo did a pretty good kaboom, too, but Lou had trouble. He performed a beautiful forward flip into the mud though, landing perfectly on his feet. It was fun to see the jumpers land on the mud and sink down. Lou received a twenty-six from the judges. Stinky received a twenty-nine and EvyPoo got a twenty-seven. Everyone cheered. Stinky, Lou and EvyPoo made their way through the mud toward the fountain.

Suddenly, out of nowhere, all six Tizer brothers came marching toward the bleachers like boy scouts in a parade. Each boy carried his loaded booty-wipe shooter on his shoulder and a backpack on his back. Three of the Tizer's went behind the right side of the fountain and the other three went behind the left side.

Before anyone had a chance to process what was happening, the Tizer boys aimed their shooters high over the heads of the contestants coming out of the mud.

"Fire!" yelled one of them.

They all started firing rolls of booty-wipe into the air toward the *Pooper's* porties. As the rolls of white tissue fell dropped, they unraveled into long strips like curtains hanging from the sky.

Everyone gasped!

"Stinky!" called Dingus to his friend who was walking toward him. "Look up!"

At once, twelve rolls of booty-wipe came tumbling all over Stinky, Lou, and EvyPoo, who were coming out of the mud pit toward the fountain. No one could believe what was happening. Mud and toilet paper do not go together well!

Then, while the jumpers were covered in mud and booty-wipe, the water on the big fountain suddenly stopped. It just stopped flowing, nothing!

Dingus and everyone in the bleachers were laughing at the mummy looking figures who were walking around trying to see through the toilet paper that covered them from head to toe. Stinky tripped over a roll of TP and saved his fall by doing a flip, tangling himself even more.

"Where's the water?" Stinky shouted to Dingus.

That was a good question. Dingus, Rhea, and Dump jumped from their seats to find out why the water was turned off.

Stinky, Lou, and EvyPoo also went looking for the water, covered in mud and booty-wipe. Unfortunately, without thinking, the three portie kids walked straight through the power drying wind tunnels! The dryers turned on automatically as they walked through the arches. Instantly, the mud and the toilet paper dried on them, turning all three of them into papier-mâché mummies!

"Aah!" they all screamed at once as they came through the arch, their voices vibrating in the wind.

It all happened so fast. Dingus was laughing so hard that he forgot about the spit wad shooters he was carrying. When he remembered, he gave one to Rhea, since Stinky could barely move.

Dingus aimed his spit wad shooter at a couple of the Tizer brothers who were reloading their booty-wipe shooters. The first spit wads went straight at Jeremy Tizer's shoulder. It took him by surprise and he dropped his shooter. The second one hit directly on Josh Tizer's trigger finger.

"Ouch!" yelled Josh, "That hurt!"

Dingus couldn't help but yell a quick, "I'm sorry!" After that, they tried not to hit them in places that might hurt.

The booty-wipe and spit wads continued to fly as Dingus and Rhea came upon Clayton who was standing on the other side of the yellow fountains. Dingus saw several hoses leading to one water spigot with three faucets on it.

"What's up Clayton?" Rhea asked Clayton.

"Nothing," Clayton said, looking down at his feet.

"Clayton, did you turn the water off?" Dingus asked as he ducked to avoid getting hit by a roll of booty-wipe.

"Uh-huh," replied Clayton quietly. "Was that bad?"

"Awe Clayton, the fountain is for the jumpers to clean the mud off." Dingus said as he turned the faucet back to the left.

At once, the water began to fall off the big rock and create a shower for the mud jumpers. More kids were coming out of the mud and getting covered with toilet paper, so the water was a big help.

Finally, Pop came running over.

"BOYS! Boys!" he yelled. Other portie parents came following up behind him.

"What's going on, guys? Why are you shooting booty-wipe at everybody?"

Jake spoke on behalf of his brothers.

"Mr. Slopp, we need to work!" said Jake, very excitedly. "We love working for Mr. Swurlee! He is a great boss. He doesn't always have the best ideas, but he pays us for each job and never lets us down. He also makes sure we always have more events to take the portables to. We cannot let *Pooper's* take all the portable potty business!"

"Jake," Pop sighed. He put his arm around the young man's shoulder. The other Tizer boys stood nearby as Pop spoke.

"Guys, listen," Pop said, looking at each of them.

"There are so many events going on all the time, there's no way *Pooper's* can handle all the business! The world needs *Superpoops* and Mr. Swurlee needs you!" Pop reassured them.

Josh, Jeremy, and the rest of the Tizer's all looked at each other. They weren't sure that Pop was telling the truth. The school bus figure-eight race was a fiasco. The manager told the boys that *Superpoops* was never going to provide portables for anyone ever again.

The boys were hoping to sabotage *Pooper's* event today. They wanted to create trouble for *Pooper's,* and they did. But it wasn't going to put *Pooper's* out of business, and *Superpoops* wasn't going to be out of business, either.

"The manager was so upset last night," Jerry Tizer explained to Pop.

"I know, I know," said Pop. "Sometimes adults say things they don't mean. Don't worry about it, guys."

"Yeah, that's right," agreed Dingus. "There is plenty of portable potty business for all of us!"

Dingus looked over at the big clock in the center of the course.
"Oh no, it's almost time for me to jump!" Dingus exclaimed.

Dingus handed his spit wad shooter to Pop and shouted to Dump and Rhea.

"Hey you guys! We gotta go! It's our turn to jump!"

"We better get over there," agreed Rhea, as she handed the spit wad shooter to a mummified Stinky.

"Let's hurry," said Dump.

"By the way, nice booty-wipe shooters!" said Dingus to the Tizer brothers. He and Stinky were going to make one for themselves, Dingus decided.

"Come with me boys, let's go watch the jumpers," said Pop to Jake Tizer and his brothers.

CHAPTER 13

JUMP FOR JOY

"And we have a winner!"

"Dingus Slopp!" Dingus heard his name being called over the loudspeaker. "Please report to the green course."

Dingus, Dump and Rhea weaved through the crowd and made their way to the entrance of the green course.

"We have been waiting for you, Dingus," said The Frog, who was getting ready to jump next. "We thought you weren't going to make it."

"You were waiting for me?" Dingus said. He was surprised The Frog even knew his name.

"Yes! Are you surprised?" The Frog replied.

"Yeah, kind of," said Dingus, shyly.

"Dude, you and your friend Stinky are famous in the trampoline world, now. You, for your tricks and Stinky for his…well, let's just say his timing is amazing! I didn't know you were Dingus Slopp when I signed your hat!"

Dingus was surprised The Frog knew who Dingus was. He thought it was funny that The Frog liked Stinky's flip and fart tricks, too. Dingus was lucky to have a funny friend like Stinky, he thought.

When it was Dingus' turn to do his tricks, he did them perfectly. His constant practicing paid off. He loved landing in the mud and sinking down, feeling the coolness on his skin. Dingus could hear the Tizer boys, Pop and the other porties up in the stands cheering for him. Dump and Rhea performed really well, also.

Dingus wished he could take a shower in the fountains every day because all that water felt so good pouring on him. Like everyone who went through the dryers, Dingus tried to talk but the wind made it pretty much impossible.

After they finished at the green course, Dingus, Dump, Rhea, and The Frog continued through the yellow and the orange course. They all did great, scoring twenty-eights and twenty-nines. On the final jump, they got to do a jump of their choice.

Rhea did a triple, Dump did a kaboom and Dingus did an original combo consisting of a triple, plus a cody. Everyone watching was astonished. They had never seen anyone do that before. Dingus had decided to try it at the last minute. He was happy it worked. The judges gave him a thirty, the first thirty of the day. Dingus was feeling pretty happy when The Frog came up and joined him under the waterfall.

"That was fire, man!" The Frog hollered at Dingus.

"Thanks!" Dingus said. Dingus never dreamed The Frog would be complimenting him.

"I wasn't sure if I was going to be able to do it, I never tried it before." Dingus admitted.

"Dude, you need to be a guest on my video and show my audience that one!"

"Sure, ok," Dingus replied, surprised.

"And you gotta get your friend Stinky to come on with us, too," The Frog said as he wiped the last bit of mud off himself. "We were watching him earlier and we couldn't stop laughing."

Dingus couldn't wait to tell Stinky what The Frog just told him. Dingus had an idea.

"Hey," he said to his new friend, "if you guys are sticking around for the awards, you could come over and have pizzas with the porties."

"Sounds like a plan, bro," said The Frog.

"There are some picnic tables behind the portables. We'll be there," said Dingus.

"Cooooool." said The Frog as he walked into the dryers, which made it sound extra cool.

The pizza showed up at the same time as The Frog did. He brought the other vloggers, including Jade "the jumping jelly bean", and Daniel, his videographer. All the porties were standing around the picnic tables. Dingus and some of the others were flipping their water bottles. They were trying to see if they could land them in a standing up position. Stinky was the only one able to do it so far.

"Here, let me try that," The Frog said to Stinky. Stinky handed The Frog his water bottle.

"Go for it!" said Stinky with a little pride in his voice. Instead of flipping the bottle like the kids were doing, The Frog did something completely different with the water. He twisted off the cap and started pouring the cold water right on Stinky's unsuspecting head.

"Wait! What?" Stinky was startled, to say the least, and jumped backward. Water was dripping from his head. He was not expecting that at all. The Frog took a step toward him and grabbed him by the waist. As Daniel videoed, Stinky tried to get away but The Frog held him tighter while still pouring the water. Everyone was laughing. He finally let Stinky go. Both boys were laughing so hard they could barely stand up.

"Dude, your flip and farts are off the chain!" The Frog said as he poured the last drops on Stinky. "You had us dying!"

"What the heck?" Stinky said, still laughing. He was surprised Daniel was videoing him.

"He's awesome, man!" The Frog said while speaking into the camera. He then pointed his finger toward Dingus as Daniel turned the camera. "And this is the amazing Dingus Slopp, who took first place today at The Flippin' Mud Festival with his crazy triple plus cody! Who does that?" Dingus shrugged his shoulders, somewhat embarrassed, then did a little bow.

"Let's eat pizza!" hollered Stinky. He grabbed some pizzas from the stack on the parent's table and put it on another table. All the kids grabbed a piece.

Everyone was laughing and enjoying their pizza when one of the portables started making a weird noise. It was creaking and making popping noises.

"Uh-oh!" said Pop with a look of worry on his face. "Is there anything we should know, Mr. Tizer?" Pop looked straight at Jake Tizer.

"I swear, we didn't do anything else!" Jake said sincerely.

Everyone looked with wonder at the portable that was making the creaking and popping noise.

Dingus and Pop walked over to it. Very slowly and carefully Pop opened the door. That's when they saw Clayton.

"Clayton Brown!" Pop shouted. "What are you doing?"

"Um, nothing?" Clayton replied, trying to sound innocent.

"Come on out of there," Pop said, a little more calmly.

Clayton walked out of the portable covered from head to toe in booty-wipe. He was carrying Josh Tizer's booty-wipe shooter on his shoulder like an army man. There was so much TP on the floor that Clayton almost tripped over it.

Daniel turned the phone and videoed Clayton. This was certainly a sight their viewers had never seen before.

"I think we need to see more of Dingus Slopp and Stinky Johns." The Frog then said to his audience. "What do you think, guys? Put your answer in the comments! Don't forget to smash the like button and subscribe! See you next time!"

As Daniel was finishing up the video, Stinky leaned in toward Daniel and pulled the phone toward himself. With his biggest smile, Stinky said,

"And if you need portable potties, call *Pooper's Portables* for the cleanest and nicest portables around!"

All at the same time, the Tizer boys hollered "*Superpoops*!" in the background.

Stinky then got up on a picnic table and performed his famous flip and fart for the world to see.

Everyone was laughing! "Turn off your smellavision!" Dingus cried through his laughter. Dingus thought this was one of the best days of his life.

About the Authors

DeNaze (Karnowski) Wharton is a grandmother with a very vivid imagination. Jacob Jones and Kayden Polidan contributed to Dingus Slopp. Jacob Jones is in the fourth grade and loves hanging out with friends, playing hockey, football, baseball, and watching and making videos. Kayden Polidan is in the second grade and loves his family, his cats, wrestling, playing video games and making videos. Favorite line: *"Pooper's* won't stand for number one!"

Made in the USA
Monee, IL
01 December 2020